SCOOBY-DOO!

BEGINNER MYSTERIES

STONE ARCH BOOKS
a capstone imprint

Published in 2017 by Stone Arch Books, A Capstone Imprint
1710 Roe Crest Drive, North Mankato, Minnesota 56003
www.mycapstone.com

ibrary of Congress Cataloging-in-Publication Data
Cataloging-in-publication information is on file with the
Library of Congress.
ISBN: 978-1-4965-4770-5 (library binding)
ISBN: 978-1-4965-4774-3 (paperback)
ISBN: 978-1-4965-4778-1 (eBook PDF)

Editorial Credits:
Editor: Alesha Sullivan
Designer: Brann Garvey
Art Director: Nathan Gassman
Media Researcher: Wanda Winch
Production Specialist: Katy LaVigne
Design Elements:
Warner Brothers design elements, 1, 4-8, 106-112
The illustrations in this book were created by Scott Jeralds

SCOOBY-DOO!

BEGINNER MYSTERIES

VAMPIRE ZOO HULLABALOO

by Michael
Anthony Steele

illustrated by
Scott Jeralds

TABLE OF CONTENTS

MEET MYSTERY INC.

SCOOBY-DOO

SKILLS: Loyal; super snout
BIO: This happy-go-lucky hound avoids scary
situations at all costs, but he'll do anything
for a Scooby Snack!

SHAGGY ROGERS

SKILLS: Lucky; healthy appetite
BIO: This laid-back dude would rather look for grub than search for clues, but he usually finds both!

FRED JONES, JR.

SKILLS: Athletic; charming
BIO: The leader and oldest member of the gang. He's a good sport — and good at them, too!

DAPHNE BLAKE

SKILLS: Brains; beauty
BIO: As a sixteen-year-old fashion queen, Daphne solves her mysteries in style.

VELMA DINKLEY

SKILLS: Clever; highly intelligent
BIO: Although she's the youngest member of Mystery Inc., Velma's an old pro at catching crooks.

CHAPTER ONE

CREEPY CREATURES

Scooby-Doo and the rest of the gang climbed out of the Mystery Machine. They looked around the empty parking lot. The setting sun made the *deserted* lot look extra creepy.

"Like, where is everyone?" asked Shaggy.

"It must be near closing time," suggested Daphne.

The Mystery Inc. gang walked across the parking lot toward the main entrance. They passed under an old sign that read *City Zoo*.

"Boy, Scott really should replace that sign," said Fred.

"I can see why your friend invited us here," said Velma. "This place looks haunted."

Shaggy and Scooby-Doo stopped in their tracks.

"A haunted zoo?" asked Shaggy.

"A raunted roo?" repeated Scooby.

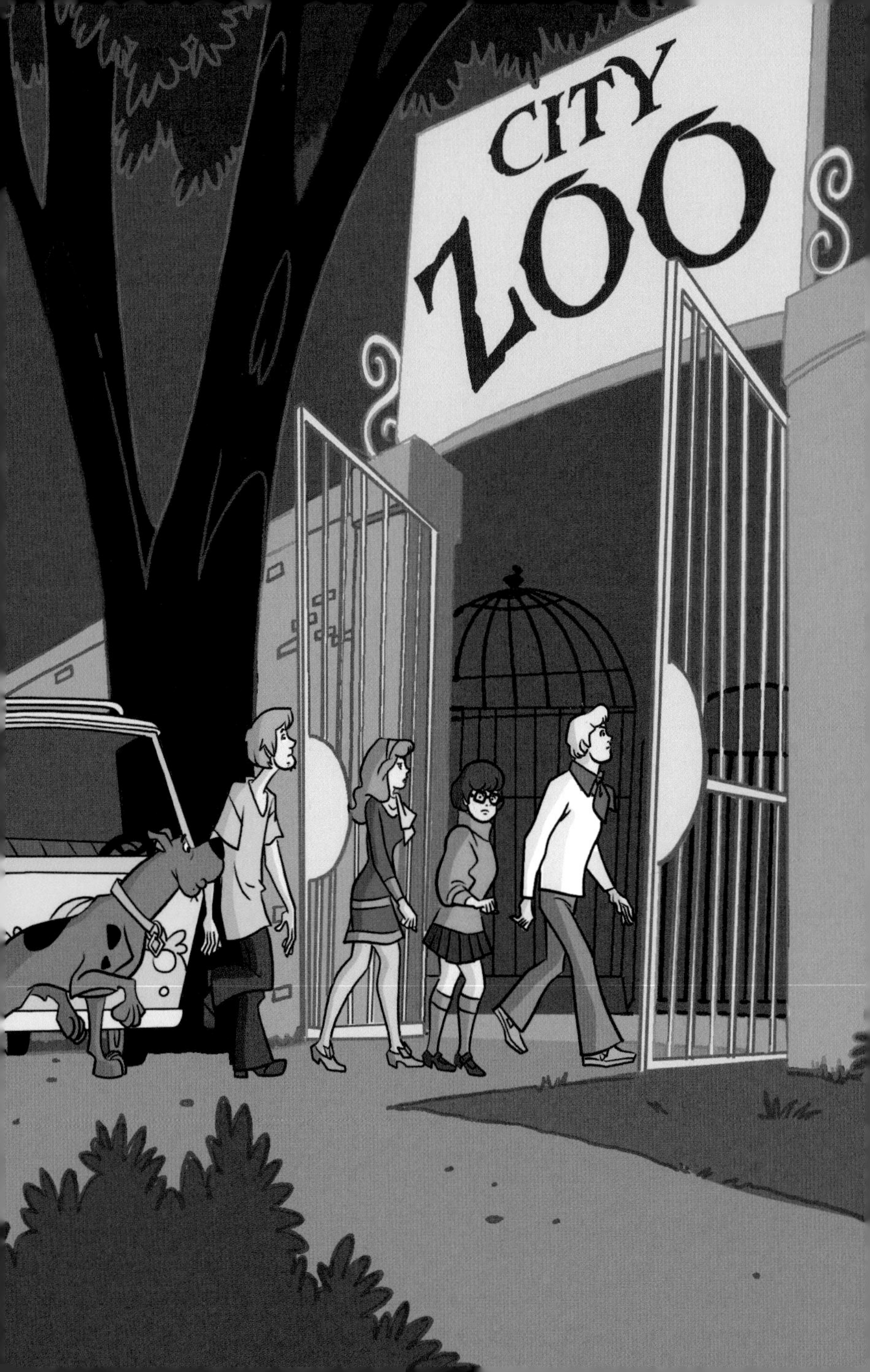
CITY
ZOO

"Like, what can be scarier than that?" asked Shaggy.

"I'm sure it's not haunted," said Fred. "My friend, Scott McFadden, said that he had a mystery that only Mystery Inc. can solve."

The gang moved toward the ticket booth, but it was empty.

"Let's go on in," suggested Fred. "Scott should be expecting us."

They stepped passed the ticket booth and entered the main zoo. There was no one in sight. No workers, no visitors, nobody. They walked past some birds in cages and some reptiles behind large glass windows.

A few different animals were in large pits surrounded by handrails. There were animals in the zoo but no people.

"I don't like the looks of this, Scoob," said Shaggy.

"Re reither," agreed Scooby.

As they moved down one of the wide pathways, a nearby bush began to move.

"What's that?" asked Velma.

The bush rustled a little longer until a man stepped out from behind it.

"Gotcha!" said the man. He pulled out a small black monkey from inside the bush.

"Hi, Scott," greeted Fred.

"You made it!" said Scott. He carried the monkey over to the gang.

"Everyone, this is Scott McFadden," said Fred.

"He just bought this old zoo from the Bohannon Circus brothers."

The rest of the gang introduced themselves.

"And I'm finding out that there's a lot to learn about running a zoo," said Scott. "Like how to keep the spider monkeys from escaping."

"Oh, he's so cute," said Daphne. She leaned closer. "May I pet him?"

"Sure, he's friendly," said Scott. "He just likes to get into trouble. Don't you, Rocco?"

As Daphne leaned in to pet him, Rocco ran up her arm and sat on her shoulder.

"I think he likes you," said Scott. "Come on, I'll give you a tour of the zoo." He waved all of them forward. "Starting with the monkey cages."

Scott led them to the monkey and apes *exhibit*. There were huge cages full of all kinds of monkeys, chimpanzees, orangutans, and even gorillas.

Scott opened one of the largest cages and held out a hand toward the spider monkey on Daphne's shoulder. "Come on, Rocco. In you go."

The monkey took Scott's hand and climbed off Daphne.

He swung into the cage, and Scott closed the door.

"Uh, excuse me, Scott," said Velma. "Am I seeing things? Or are those chimpanzees playing cards?" She pointed to a small table in the chimpanzee cage. Four chimps sat around a table, each holding several playing cards.

"Wow," said Fred. "I guess you can take the chimp out of the circus but you can't take the circus out of the chimp."

Scott laughed. "Most of my zoo animals were taken from a circus where they were being *mistreated*."

One of the chimpanzees slammed his winning cards onto the table. The other chimps shook their heads and threw down their losing cards.

"That reminds me," said Scott. "You're going to love this." He led the group to another part of the zoo. Everyone stepped up to a handrail overlooking a large open pit filled with trees, bushes, and rocks. A large grizzly bear sat on a rock and scratched his stomach.

Scott opened a nearby shed and pulled out a unicycle. It looked like a bicycle but with only one wheel.

Scott leaned over the railing. "Hey, Bobo! Heads up!"

Scott tossed down the unicycle, and the big brown bear caught it with both paws. He looked at it for a moment and then put the wheel on the ground. The bear hopped on and began pedaling around his pen.

"Like, that's so cool," said Shaggy.

"It is," agreed Fred. "But I'm guessing that's not why you asked us here. Is it?"

"It's not," replied Scott. "For one thing, something has been scaring away all of the workers and visitors."

Shaggy gulped. "Like, what?"

"I don't know," said Scott. "Besides that, animals have been disappearing from their cages."

"That is a mystery," said Velma.

"Let me show you the latest." Scott led them to a smaller cage nearby. Its door was wide open, and the cage was empty.

"What was in this little cage?" asked Daphne.

"This used to house two vampire bats," explained Scott.

"V-v-v-v-v-v-v-v-v …" stuttered Shaggy.

"Rid he say rampire?" asked Scooby-Doo.

"Like, it's already dark," said Shaggy. He looked around and shivered. "Since vampires only come out at night, there could be some roaming around right now!"

"Don't be silly, Shaggy," said Velma. "That's just the name of these kinds of bats. They don't really turn into vampires."

"They don't?" asked Shaggy.

"No, they don't," replied Scott.

"Spider monkeys and vampire bats," said Shaggy. "With names like that, no wonder people are scared away."

"I don't think that's it," said Scott. "But I could use your help looking for the bats. I have to feed the animals right now, but then I can join you."

"We'd be happy to help!" said Daphne.

"Ooh! I can think of two animals that could use feeding right now," said Shaggy. He and Scooby each pointed to their open mouths.

Scott laughed. "You're welcome to help yourself at the snack bar."

"You can count on us, Scott," said Fred. "Let's split up to cover more ground."

"And maybe we can find some clues along the way," added Velma.

CHAPTER TWO

DO NOT FEED THE ANIMALS

Shaggy and Scooby-Doo walked down a dark pathway. They passed several animal exhibits. Some zoo animals slept while others waited for Scott to deliver their dinner.

Shaggy shined his flashlight into the treetops. "I never thought I'd say this but … like, here batty-batty-bat."

"Bats are creepy," said Shaggy. "But the sooner we find them, the sooner we can solve this mystery."

They traveled further down the path until Shaggy's flashlight beam landed on something better than missing vampire bats.

"Bingo!" shouted Shaggy.

"Rou rind the bats?" asked Scooby-Doo.

"Better than that, pal of mine," replied Shaggy. "I found the snack bar!"

Shaggy and Scooby ran up to the small shed. Shaggy opened the door and leaned inside. He came out with two bags of peanuts.

"Like, I think we could use a snack break," said Shaggy. He handed a bag to Scooby.

"Reah! Reah!" agreed Scooby-Doo.

Shaggy and Scooby sat on a bench near a sign that read *Please Do Not Feed the Animals*.

Shaggy pulled out a peanut and tossed it toward his open mouth. The peanut took a sharp turn and disappeared into the bushes behind them. Scooby-Doo tossed up a nut, and it flew into the bushes too.

Shaggy tried again, but the nut flew off into the bushes once more. He gulped. "Like, maybe this place is haunted after all."

Just then, something long and gray snaked out from the bushes behind them. The end of the long tube pointed at Shaggy's bag of peanuts.

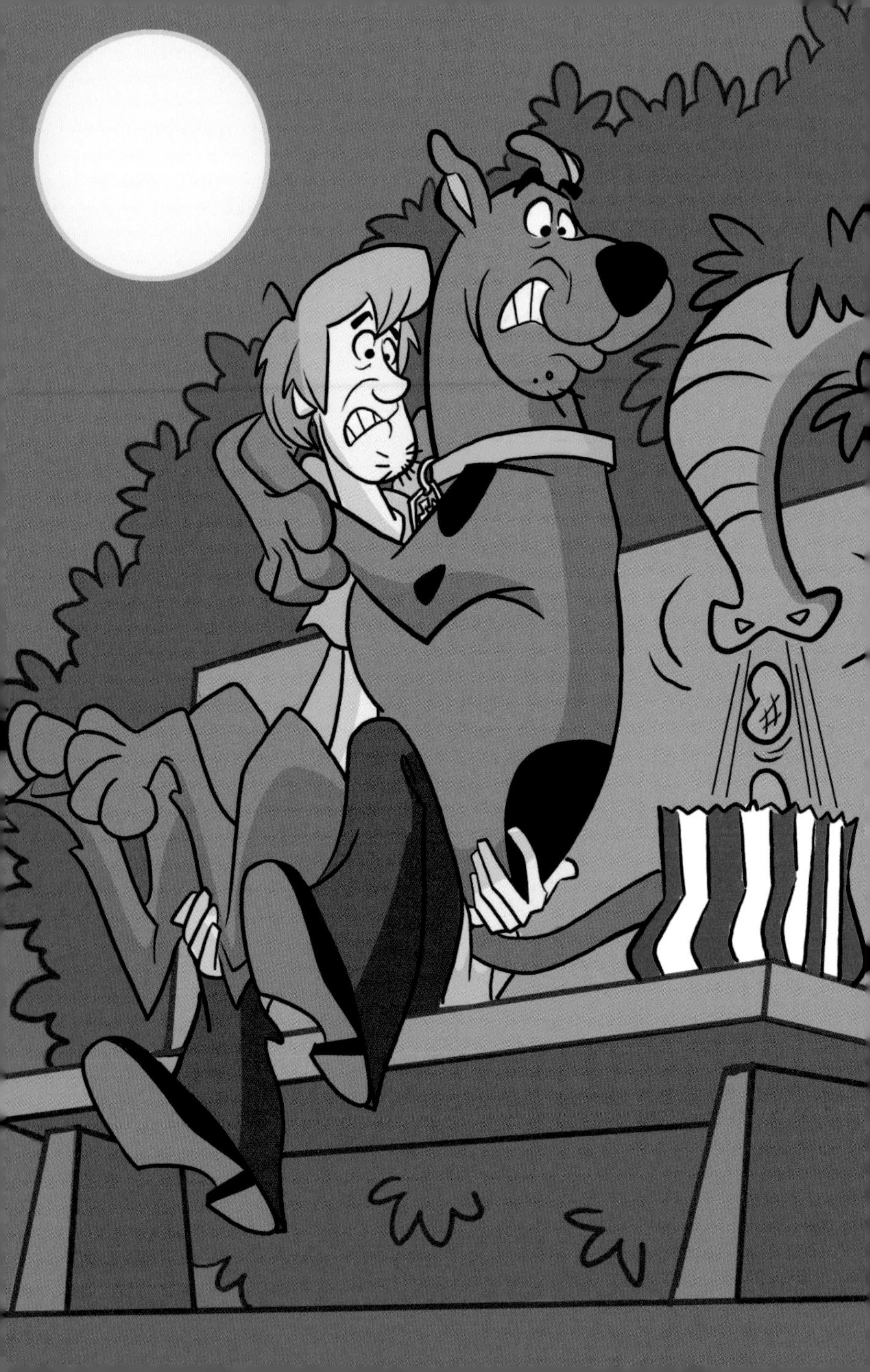

Like a vacuum hose, it sucked all the peanuts out of the bag. Then it disappeared back into the bushes.

"Zoinks!" shouted Shaggy. He jumped up and landed in Scooby's arms.

Tk-tk-tk-tk-tk-tk! Their teeth chattered.

The bushes shook and then parted. A baby elephant stepped into the light.

Fffffft! It gave a small trumpet with its long trunk.

Shaggy hopped down from Scooby-Doo's arms. "Check it out, Scoob. It's just a baby elephant."

Shaggy walked over and pat the elephant on the head. "How did you get out, little guy?"

"He rikes reanuts too," said Scooby-Doo.

Shaggy pointed to the nearby sign. "I guess elephants can't read."

Fffffff! The elephant trumpeted again. Then it turned and disappeared through the bushes.

"Let's get this little fella back to his cage," suggested Shaggy.

Shaggy pulled back the bushes and aimed his flashlight. The elephant was gone.

Shaggy shined the flashlight all over. There was no sign of the baby elephant.

Scooby poked his head through the bushes. "Rhere did it ro?!!"

"I don't know, buddy," replied Shaggy. "Like, how can an elephant just disappear?"

Ha-ha-ha-ha-ha-ha!

A creepy laugh echoed through the trees.

Shaggy gulped. "Elephants don't make creepy laughs, do they, Scoob?"

Scooby trembled. "Ruh-uh. Ruh … uh!"

Shaggy and Scooby slowly turned back to the walkway. They saw a dark figure floating down the path toward them. Its black robe swirled as it hovered just above the ground.

The creature had a pale face, two piercing red eyes, and two sharp fangs jutting from its mouth.

Ha-ha-ha-ha-ha-ha!

The creature laughed as it floated closer with its arms outstretched.

Shaggy and Scooby-Doo hugged each other and shuddered.

"Like, I know Velma said vampire bats don't really turn into vampires," said Shaggy.

"But that sure looks like a vampire
to me."

"Reah! Reah!" agreed Scooby.

CHAPTER THREE

OUT ON A LIMB

Daphne, Velma, and Fred all searched a different part of the zoo. Fred and Daphne used flashlights to search the treetops for the missing vampire bats. Velma kept her flashlight pointed at the path in front of them.

"Those bats are going to be hard to spot way up in the trees," said Fred.

"While you two look for the bats, I'll look for clues," said Velma. She stopped in her tracks. "And I think I just found something."

Velma aimed her flashlight at a folded piece of paper on the ground. Fred and Daphne gathered around while Velma picked it up and unfolded it.

"Is that a map of the zoo?" asked Daphne.

"I think so," replied Velma. "It looks like something they would sell in the gift shop."

Fred pointed to parts of the map. "It looks as if someone wrote all over this one."

"The elephant pit is circled," said Daphne. "So are the bear and monkey exhibits."

"A bunch of them are circled," said Velma. She smiled. "I think we just found our first clue."

Something rustled in the tree above them. All three shined their flashlights into the branches. A little black monkey swung from branch to branch.

"It's Rocco," said Daphne. "He must've escaped again."

Fred held up a hand. "Come here, Rocco," he said. "Come on down."

The little monkey shook his head and clamped onto one of the branches. He wasn't coming down.

"Here." Daphne handed Fred her flashlight. Then she grabbed the lowest branch. "He likes me, remember?" She began to climb the tree.

"Be careful, Daphne," warned Velma.

Daphne made her way up the tree until she was next to the monkey. She reached out a hand. "Hi, little guy," she greeted. "Remember me?"

Rocco took her outstretched hand and swung onto her shoulder. He chattered happily.

Daphne looked at the branch below her. "Now I just have to find my way down."

KRAK!

The branch snapped. Rocco held tight to Daphne's head as she fell. Someone caught her just before she hit the ground.

"Thanks for the save, Fred," said Daphne.

"Uh, Daphne," said Fred. "I'm over here."

Daphne saw that Fred and Velma were hiding behind the trunk of the large tree. Daphne looked down at the arms that held her.

They were huge and covered
with black fur. Rocco sprang from
Daphne's shoulder, as she turned
face-to-face with a huge gorilla.

Daphne smiled, trying to remain
calm. "Uh, guys? There's a big
gorilla holding me."

"We know," said Velma. "It came
out of nowhere!"

The gorilla tilted his head, looking Daphne over.

Velma spotted a large basket of fruit. "Look," she said. "This must be what Scott feeds some of the animals. Let's *distract* the gorilla."

"Good idea," said Fred.

They each grabbed a handful of fruit and tossed some at the gorilla. A large apple bonked the back of its head. The gorilla looked back at them.

"It's working," said Fred. "Keep it up."

As they whacked the ape with more fruit, the gorilla sat Daphne on the ground. Then it turned to face its attackers. The gorilla caught a flying apple, an orange, and a banana in midair. Fred and Velma stopped throwing fruit.

"Now what?" asked Velma.

The gorilla looked at Fred and Velma and then at the fruit in its hands. A wide grin stretched across its face and it began to … juggle the fruit!

"Whoa!" shouted Fred.

"He must be one of the former circus animals," said Velma.

The gorilla caught all the fruit in one hand and took a bow.

Fred and Velma clapped.

Daphne joined them. "That was amazing!"

"I guess we better find Scott and let him know that his gorilla is loose," said Fred.

Velma looked around. "Where did he go?"

Everyone scanned the area, but the gorilla and Rocco were gone.

"They were just right here," said Daphne. "How could they have disappeared?"

Ha-ha-ha-ha-ha-ha!

"What was that?" asked Fred.

Daphne shivered. "A creepy laugh in the middle of a dark zoo?"

"Jinkies!" shouted Velma. "Look!" She pointed to a dark figure flying down the path toward them.

Ha-ha-ha-ha-ha-ha!

The figure laughed as it swooped toward the gang.

"A vampire!" yelled Fred. "Run!"

CHAPTER FOUR

FRIGHTFUL FLIGHT

Shaggy and Scooby-Doo ran down one of the dark pathways. The vampire floated behind them. Shaggy and Scooby turned a corner and lunged behind a park bench. They shivered and hugged each other as the vampire flew by.

"Like, we need a better place to hide, Scoob," whispered Shaggy.

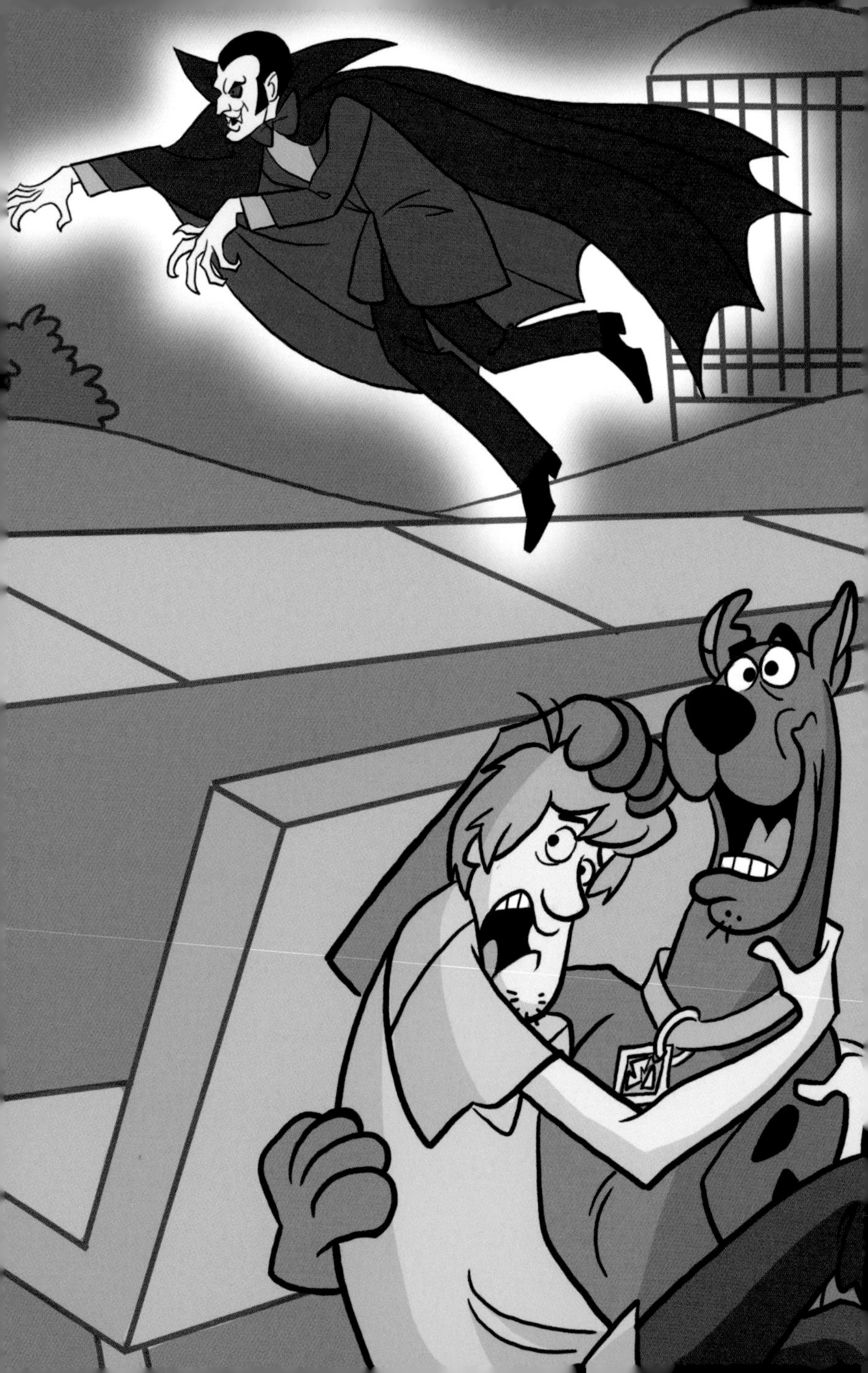

"Reah," agreed Scooby. "But rhere?"

Shaggy looked around. "I think I found something. Come on."

The vampire's pale face looked back and forth trying to find the frightened friends. Shaggy and Scooby picked up the park bench and tiptoed across the path. When the monster was out of sight, Shaggy and Scooby sprinted to a nearby *storage* shed.

"In here, pal," said Shaggy.

Shaggy opened the shed door. A pile of brightly colored *costumes* poured out. Shaggy was buried under a mound of cloth.

He struggled to the top only to have his head stuck in a cartoon lion mask.

Scooby covered his mouth, trying not to laugh.

"Like, that's not funny, Scoob," said Shaggy as he pulled off the mask.

Scooby-Doo snickered. "Rorry."

"But this does give me an idea," said Shaggy. He dug through the pile of costumes. "Here, help me out."

When the vampire floated back to the shed, Shaggy and Scooby were gone. He glided over to the handrail overlooking a nearby animal pit. The vampire peered over the edge but only saw a bunch of penguins waddling around. However, two of the penguins were much larger than the others.

"Like, no one will find us here," whispered Shaggy as he waddled in his penguin costume. "Oops."

He bit his lip. "I forgot. Penguins can't talk."

Scooby-Doo shook his head. The beak on his penguin costume went back and forth. "A ralking animal," whispered Scooby. "Rat's silly."

The vampire leaned over the railing. He was unsure of the two oversized penguins. Suddenly the monster ducked down. Someone unlocked the door in the back of the penguin exhibit.

"All right, rockhoppers!" said Scott. He held a bucket full of fish. "Time for dinner!"

All of the penguins padded their way toward Scott.

Shaggy and Scooby waddled along with them. Scott began tossing small fish out to the penguins. Each bird caught a fish and swallowed it whole.

Shaggy glanced up at the railing. The vampire was still there, peeking over the side. "Like, the vampire is still watching us, Scoob," he whispered. "But I sure don't want to swallow one of those stinky, raw fish."

Scooby shook his head. "Ruh-uh. Me reither!"

As Scooby and Shaggy waddled closer, Scott held out a fish.

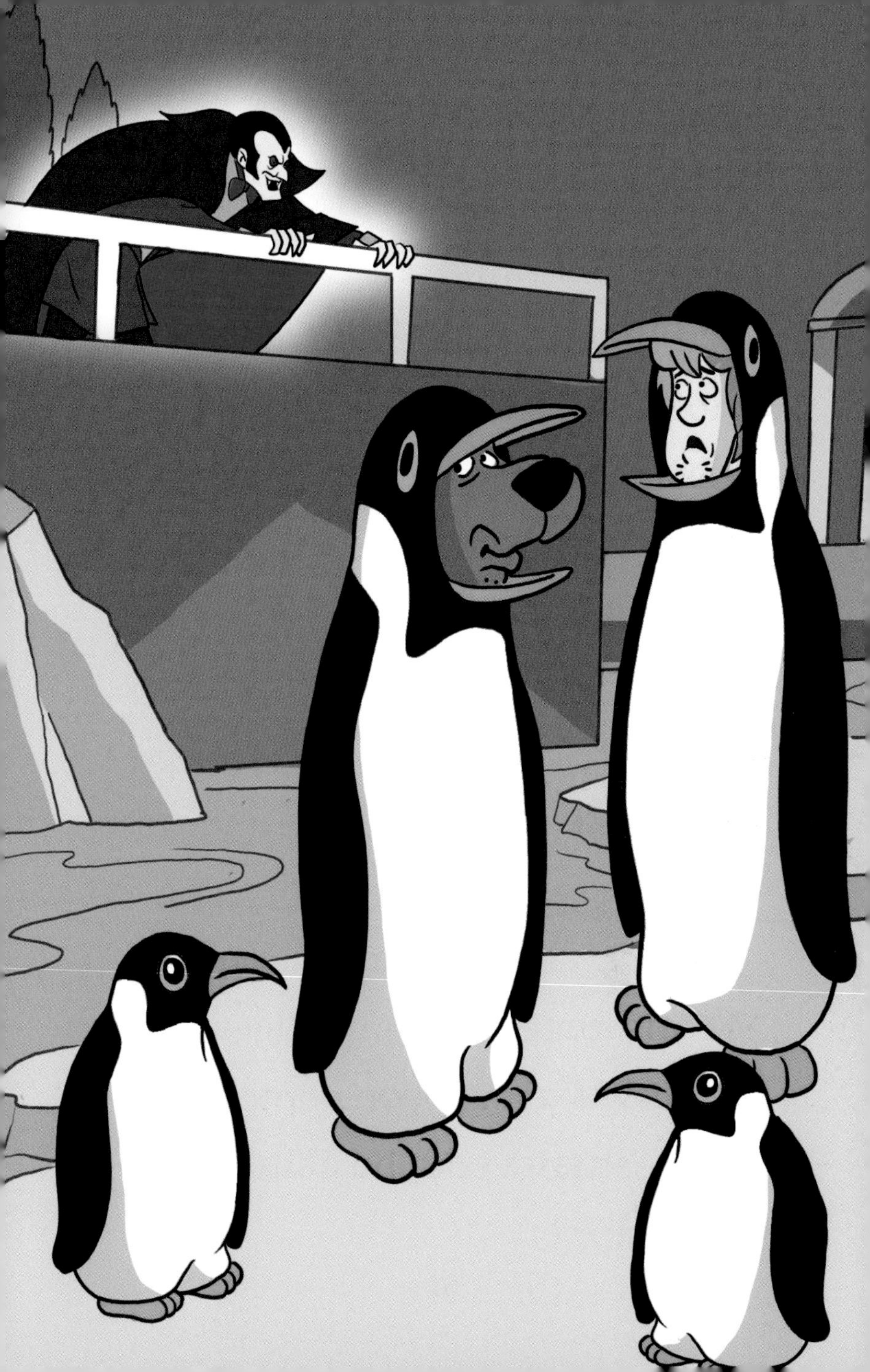

"Boy, you two are big ones," he said. "Here's your dinner."

Shaggy and Scooby both shook their heads. Their penguin beaks went back and forth.

Scott pushed the fish closer to them. "Aw, come on. You know you want to."

Shaggy rubbed his penguin belly with one of his penguin fins. "Like, no thank you. We're still full from lunch."

"Reah," agreed Scooby-Doo.

Scott leaned closer. "Shaggy? Scooby? What are you doing in here?" Shaggy pointed a fin up at the vampire.

"Like, hiding from him!" yelled Shaggy.

The vampire rose above the handrail and pointed at them.

"A vampire?!!" shouted Scott.

"Like, let's get out of here!" screamed Shaggy. He dashed toward a large slide in the center of the ice.

"Rimb on!" said Scooby-Doo. He pulled Scott onto his back and flew onto the slide after Shaggy.

With Scott on Scooby's back, they slid down the long, icy hill. The *ramp* at the bottom sent them all soaring into the air. Shaggy and Scooby held out their fins as they sailed toward the vampire.

The vampire quickly floated away
into the bushes.

BAM! KRASH!

Scott, Shaggy, and Scooby landed
above the pit near the handrail.

"Come on," yelled Shaggy.
"We have to warn the others about
the vampire!"

CHAPTER FIVE

Fred, Daphne, and Velma hid behind a large row of bushes. They watched the vampire float back and forth across a grassy picnic area. The Mystery Inc. gang did their best to keep quiet as they waited for the monster to leave.

Daphne gasped. "Look," she whispered.

A second vampire glided into view. The two monsters circled each other, searching for the gang.

"Two vampires," whispered Fred. "Just like there are two missing vampire bats."

"There has to be more to it," whispered Velma. "Vampire bats don't turn into actual vampires."

"Well, I'm not going to ask them to find out," whispered Daphne.

The gang stayed hidden while the vampires continued to drift around the area. After a while, the two monsters floated away. Fred, Velma, and Daphne climbed out of the bushes.

"I hope we've seen the last of those vampires," said Daphne.

"Me too," agreed Fred. "Now we need to track down the missing gorilla and Scott's other missing animals."

"Speaking of tracks," said Velma. "I think I found another clue."

She shined her flashlight onto the ground.

"Tire tracks," said Daphne.

"These look like bicycle tires," said Velma.

"Let's follow them and see where they go," suggested Fred.

With Velma in the lead, the gang followed the tracks through the zoo. They passed several animal cages and exhibits. Some cages held sleeping animals, but many of them were empty.

They followed the tracks to a landing that overlooked an animal pen.

Before they could see what was below, Daphne placed a hand on Velma's shoulder.

"Turn off the flashlight," whispered Daphne.

Velma switched off the light just as a vampire appeared on the pathway behind them. The monster turned his head from side to side, still searching.

"He hasn't spotted us yet," whispered Fred. "Let's hide."

As they turned to run, the second vampire appeared on the path.

"There's nowhere to hide!" cried Velma.

"I have an idea," said Fred.

The two vampires floated toward each other. They sailed past each other, continuing their search. Neither vampire saw the pair of hands holding onto the other side of the handrail.

Fred held tight to the railing while he dangled over the exhibit below. Velma held onto his legs, and Daphne held onto Velma's legs.

Daphne looked down into the dark water below. "I don't know what lives down there," she whispered. "But I hope it's friendly."

Just then, an alligator leaped out of the water.

Daphne pulled up her legs just as it tried to take a bite.

SNAP!

Another alligator circled below. Daphne pulled her legs up just in time again.

SNAP! SNAP!

"Fred," Daphne whispered as loud as she dared. "I have a situation down here!"

Fred held tight as he watched the vampires float away. "Just a minute, Daphne," he whispered. "They're almost gone."

A third alligator leaped out of the water. Daphne kept swinging her legs away from the snapping jaws.

SNAP! SNAP! SNAP!

"I'm going to be gone if we wait another minute," Daphne said.

SNAP-SNAP-SNAP! SNAP-SNAP!

Fred lifted himself over the handrail. He helped Velma climb up after him. Then they both pulled up Daphne.

"That was a great hiding spot if I do say so myself," said Fred.

Daphne sighed and blew a strand of hair away from her face. Velma switched on her flashlight. "Come on. Let's finish tracking those tracks!"

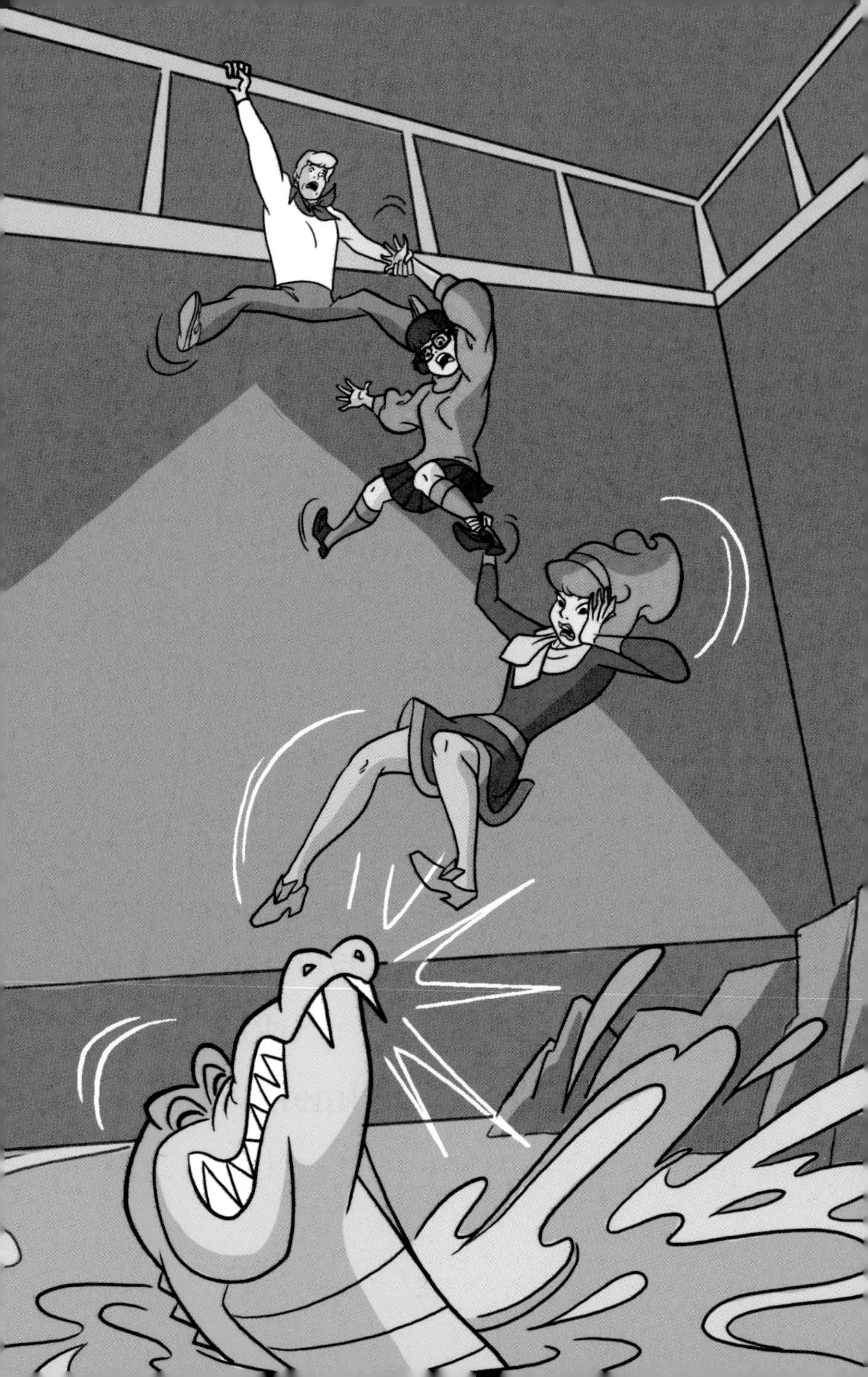

CHAPTER SIX

UPROAR

Shaggy and Scooby-Doo followed Scott toward a long building attached to several large cages. They passed under a sign reading *Big Cats*.

Scooby-Doo looked up at the sign. "Ruh-roh."

"I can't believe we haven't found the others yet," said Scott.

Shaggy ran ahead to the first door he could find. "Like, I say we hide out in this closet until this all blows over."

"Shaggy, wait!" yelled Scott.

It was too late. Shaggy opened the door and was buried under a pile of unicycles, juggling pins, and colorful balls.

"Hee-hee-hee-hee-hee-hee," giggled Scooby.

Shaggy climbed out of the mound. "Like, I think you have some storage problems around here."

Scott shrugged. "Like I said, a bunch of these animals came from the circus. Now I'm up to my elbows in circus stuff."

Scooby tapped Shaggy on the shoulder. "R-R-R-R-Raggy, rook!" He pointed to the two vampires gliding up the pathway.

"Yipes! And double yipes!" shouted Shaggy. "Now there are two vampires! Like, we gotta hide!"

Scott ran down the side of the building while Shaggy and Scooby-Doo jumped into the closet. Scooby grabbed the doorknob with his tail and slammed the door shut behind them.

The vampires floated up to the door. They looked at each other, and then one reached for the doorknob. They hissed when the door flew open.

Shaggy jumped out wearing tan shorts and a tan shirt.

"Careful!" warned Shaggy. "Dangerous lion on the loose!"

Scooby stepped out of the closet. He wore an old mop atop his head like a lion's mane. Scooby growled and pretended to claw at the vampires. The monsters looked at each other and then back to Scooby and Shaggy. They floated closer.

"I don't think they're buying it, Scoob," whispered Shaggy. "Give them a roar."

Scooby-Doo planted his feet on the ground and opened his mouth wide.

ROOOOOOOOOOAAAAAAR!

The vampires flew back in surprise and slammed into each other. Then they sped away back toward the pathway.

"That showed them," said Shaggy. "Great job, buddy!"

"But, Raggy," said Scooby-Doo. "Rhat rasn't me."

"What do you mean that wasn't you?!!" asked Shaggy.

ROOOOOOOOOOAAAAAAR!

Shaggy and Scooby turned to see a real lion standing behind them.

"Zoinks!" shouted Shaggy. He jumped into Scooby's arms.

"It's okay," said Scott. He held onto the lion's leash. "This is Harambee. He's from a circus too."

Harambee leaned forward and gave Shaggy's face a big lick.

Shaggy laughed nervously. "Like, as long as he's not picturing us as two T-bone steaks."

Scott laughed. "Let me put him back in his cage and we can find the others."

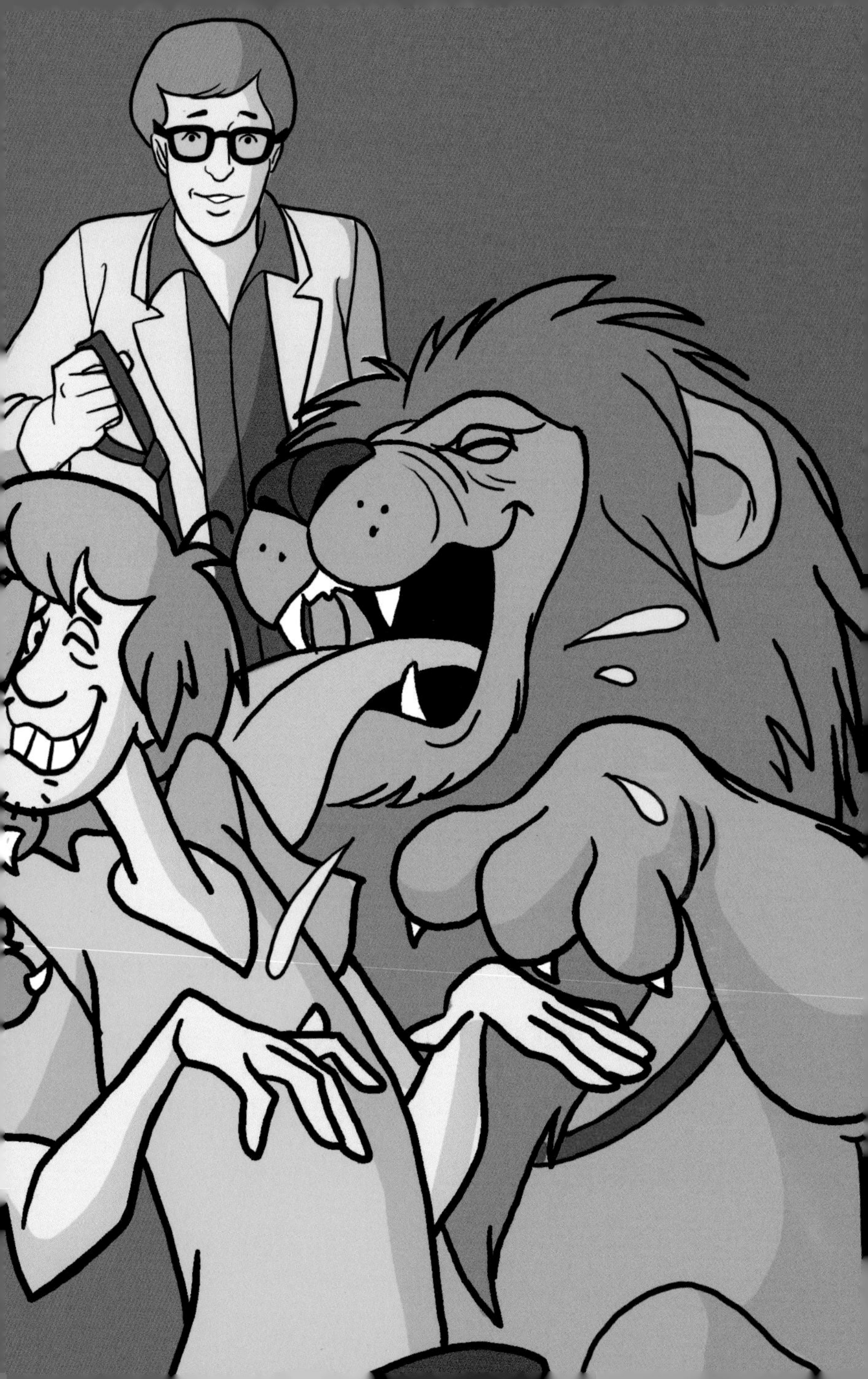

#
CAGEY DISCOVERY

Velma, Daphne, and Fred followed the thin tire tracks to the back of the zoo. They stopped in front of a wall of bushes and tree branches.

Velma aimed her flashlight at the thick brush. "That doesn't make any sense," she said. "The tracks stop right here."

"Where do we go from here?" asked Daphne.

Fred frowned as he looked at the wall of greenery. "There's no way around. It's a dead end."

Daphne pulled at one of the small tree limbs. "Hey, look. This branch has been cut."

Fred leaned closer. "This is just a big pile of brush." He pulled away some more branches. "Let's clear this out and see where these tracks lead."

As he and Daphne began moving branches, Velma switched off the flashlight.

"Hey, where's the light?" asked Daphne.

"Do you hear that?" whispered Velma.

"Footsteps ..." said Daphne. "Someone's coming!"

"Quick, hide!" said Fred.

Fred, Daphne, and Velma ducked behind a nearby tree. The footsteps grew louder and louder. Shaggy, Scooby, and Scott ran down the path.

"I thought I saw a flashlight over here," said Scott. "But I don't see anyone."

"Scott?" Fred stepped out from behind the tree. "Is that you?"

"There you are, Fred!" said Scott.

"Like, we've been looking all over for you," said Shaggy. "We've been running and hiding from a couple of creepy vampires."

"Us too," said Daphne. "We barely had time to look for clues."

"And we were just about to see where these tire tracks lead before you showed up," added Velma.

Everyone worked together to pull away the cut branches. When the brush was cleared, two doors stood before them.

"That's not supposed to be there," said Scott.

"They look like the doors on the back of a semitrailer," said Velma.

"Let's open them and see," suggested Fred.

Fred and Shaggy opened the doors and saw that it was the back of a trailer. And the trailer was full of different-sized cages. The cages were full of animals.

Shaggy pointed to a large cage. "Like, that's the baby elephant we saw."

"Reah, reah!" agreed Scooby-Doo.

Daphne pointed to the cage next to the elephant. "And I'd recognize that juggling gorilla anywhere."

"It's all the missing animals," gasped Scott. He pointed to a cage containing two little bats. "Including the vampire bats."

"Like, someone has been
stashing them here the entire time,"
said Shaggy.

"I better get all of these
animals back to their proper
places," said Scott.

Velma tapped her chin. "I think
it's time to cage some vampires!"

78

CHAPTER EIGHT

PLAN B

Shaggy and Scooby-Doo walked down one of the zoo's main trails. They looked around, expecting the vampires to come out at any moment.

"Like, just once I'd like Fred to come up with a plan where we aren't the *bait*," said Shaggy.

"Rou said it," agreed Scooby.

Fred stood atop the roof of a nearby building. He scanned the area with *binoculars*. He could see most of the zoo from where he stood.

Fred zoomed in to make sure Daphne and Velma were in place for his plan. But so far, there was no sign of the vampires.

Back on the ground, Shaggy and Scooby kept walking.

"Like, maybe those creepy vampires decided to give up," suggested Shaggy.

"No such ruck," said Scooby-Doo.

Shaggy and Scooby spotted the two vampires floating across the pathway ahead.

"I can't believe I'm going to do this," said Shaggy. He waved his arms in the air. "Yoo-hoo! Creepy vampires!"

The vampires turned their glowing red eyes toward Shaggy. The monsters flew straight at him and Scooby.

"Come on, Scoob," Shaggy yelled as he began to run. "Feet don't fail me now!"

"Reah," agreed Scooby-Doo. "Me reither!"

The two ran as fast as they could away from the vampires. But the monsters quickly caught up to them.

"Okay, Scoob," said Shaggy. "Time for our secret weapon."

Shaggy and Scooby dived into the bushes. They burst out of the other side, each riding a unicycle. They pedaled quickly as the vampires continued to chase them.

"This'll give us some speed, huh, Scoob?" asked Shaggy.

"Reah," agreed Scooby-Doo. "Raster, raster!"

Shaggy and Scooby led the vampires straight to the monkey exhibit.

"Get ready, Velma!" shouted Fred.

Velma hid behind a small group of trees. She held a thick rope in both hands. "Ready!" she replied.

Shaggy and Scooby pedaled toward the trees. The vampires were close behind them. When Shaggy and Scooby were under the trees, Fred yelled down at Velma. "Now!"

Velma pulled on the large rope. Just then Shaggy's unicycle hit a rock.

"Zoinks!" Shaggy tumbled to the ground and landed under the trees.

The vampires flew past Shaggy as the giant cage fell down from the trees. Shaggy was trapped, but the vampires were still free — and angry.

Shaggy stood and grabbed the bars of the cage.

"Like, at least I'm not trapped in here with a couple of creepy vampires."

"On, no," said Fred. He cupped his hands around his mouth and shouted down, "Plan B!"

Scooby-Doo whimpered as the vampires still chased him. Velma pulled up beside him on her own unicycle. "This way, Scoob," she said.

Velma and Scooby-Doo turned down the path leading toward the Big Cats exhibit.

"Get ready, Daphne!" shouted Fred.

Daphne was hiding with a rope of her own. She held it with both hands and got ready.

The vampires floated closer as Velma and Scooby neared the long building.

"Okay, Scooby," said Velma. "Remember the plan. Get ready to turn left."

"Right," agreed Scooby.

"Not right," Velma corrected. "Left."

"Right," Scooby-Doo agreed again. "Reft!"

"Great," said Velma. "Now I'm confused."

"Now, Daphne!" Fred shouted from above.

Scooby-Doo turned left and Velma turned right. The vampires floated after Scooby while Velma turned right into Fred's trap. Daphne pulled her rope, and a huge net scooped Velma off the ground.

Scooby-Doo looked around. "Relma? Relma?" All he could see was the two dark figures chasing him.

Scooby gulped. "Ruh-roh!"

CHAPTER NINE

PLAN Z

Scooby-Doo pedaled faster and faster. He zipped around corners and zigzagged around trees, but the vampires continued to race after him.

Ha-ha-ha-ha-ha-ha!

The monsters laughed as they sailed closer.

"Raggy?" asked Scooby-Doo. "Raphne? Relma? Ranybody?!!"

Scott joined Fred up on the roof. "How's it going, Fred?"

"Not good at all," said Fred. "We just bungled Plan B, and we don't have a Plan C."

"I have an idea," said Scott. "We're in a zoo. So how about a Plan Z?"

The gang watched the vampires continue to chase Scooby through the park. Scooby pedaled as fast as he could. He whimpered as the vampires floated closer and closer. They closed in, reaching out for him. Scooby shut his eyes tight.

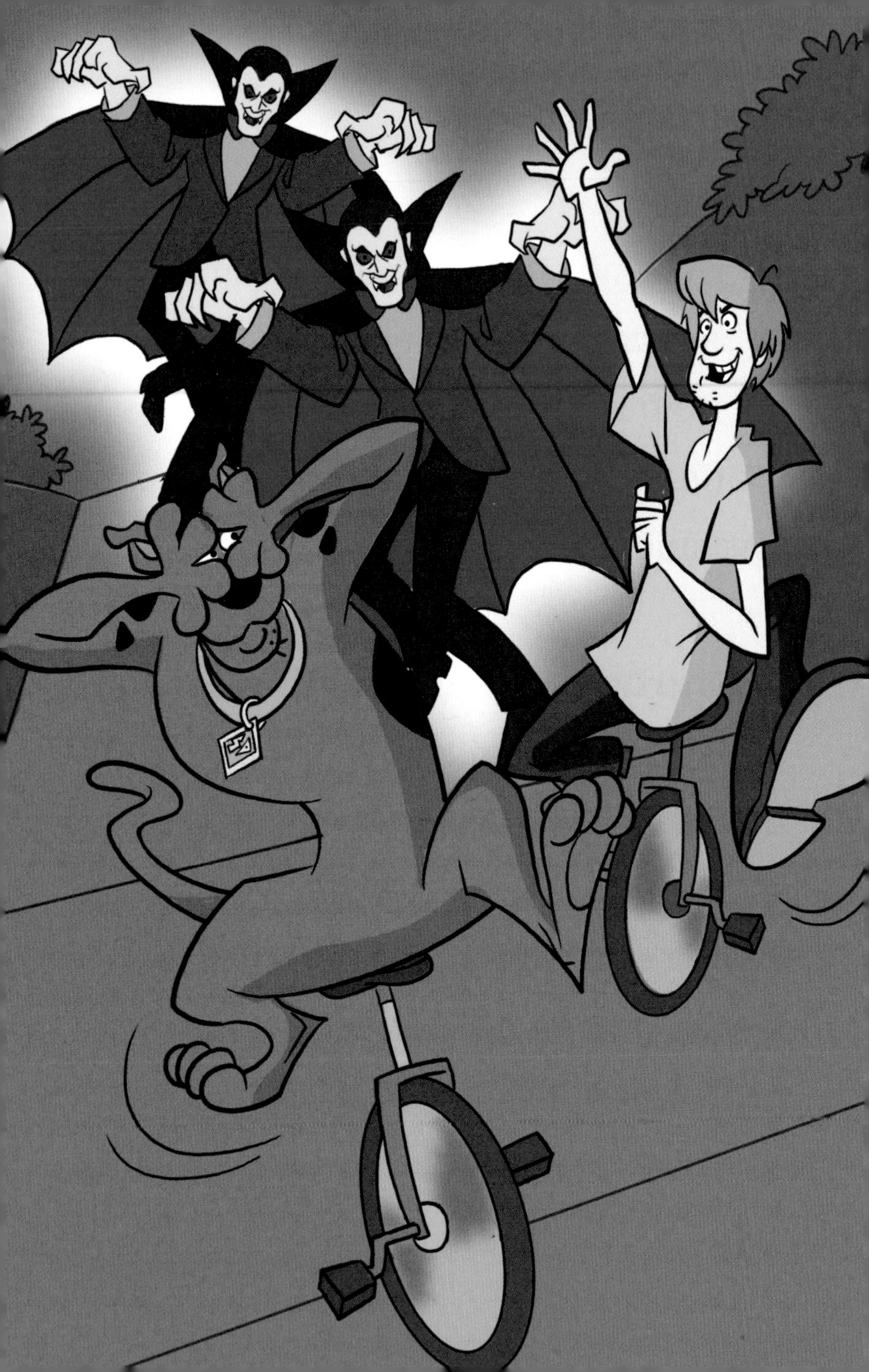

"Don't worry, Scoob," said a voice beside him.

Scooby-Doo opened his eyes to see Shaggy riding a unicycle beside him.

"Like, time for Plan Z, pal," said Shaggy. "Follow me!"

The two turned left down a different path. Up ahead, they saw a row of elephants on each side of the trail. As they got closer, each elephant dipped its trunk into a large bucket of water.

When Shaggy and Scooby led the vampires past the elephants, the animals blasted the vampires with streams of water.

The vampires coughed and
sputtered as they pushed through
the water.

"Like, that should soften them
up," said Shaggy. "Huh, Scoob?"

"Reah!" agreed Scooby-Doo.
He giggled. "Hee-hee-hee-hee-hee!"

Just then, Fred and Velma
pulled up on unicycles beside
Shaggy and Scooby.

"This way, gang," said Fred.
He led them down another path.

The vampires were soaked and
angry. They chased after the gang
with blazing red eyes.

Fred and Velma led the monsters
to a trail lined with animals.
Different kinds of apes stood on
each side of the path. There were
chimpanzees, orangutans, and
gorillas … juggling fruit!

"I think we'd better duck," warned Velma.

Scooby-Doo and the gang ducked down as they pedaled forward. All of the apes began throwing fruit at the vampires. The monsters grunted and swerved as they were *bombarded*.

Scooby reached up and grabbed a flying apple. He took a bite.

"Rooby-rooby-doo!"

As the gang left the apes behind, the vampires still followed. Shaggy looked over his shoulder and gulped. "Like, these two just don't give up!"

CHAPTER TEN

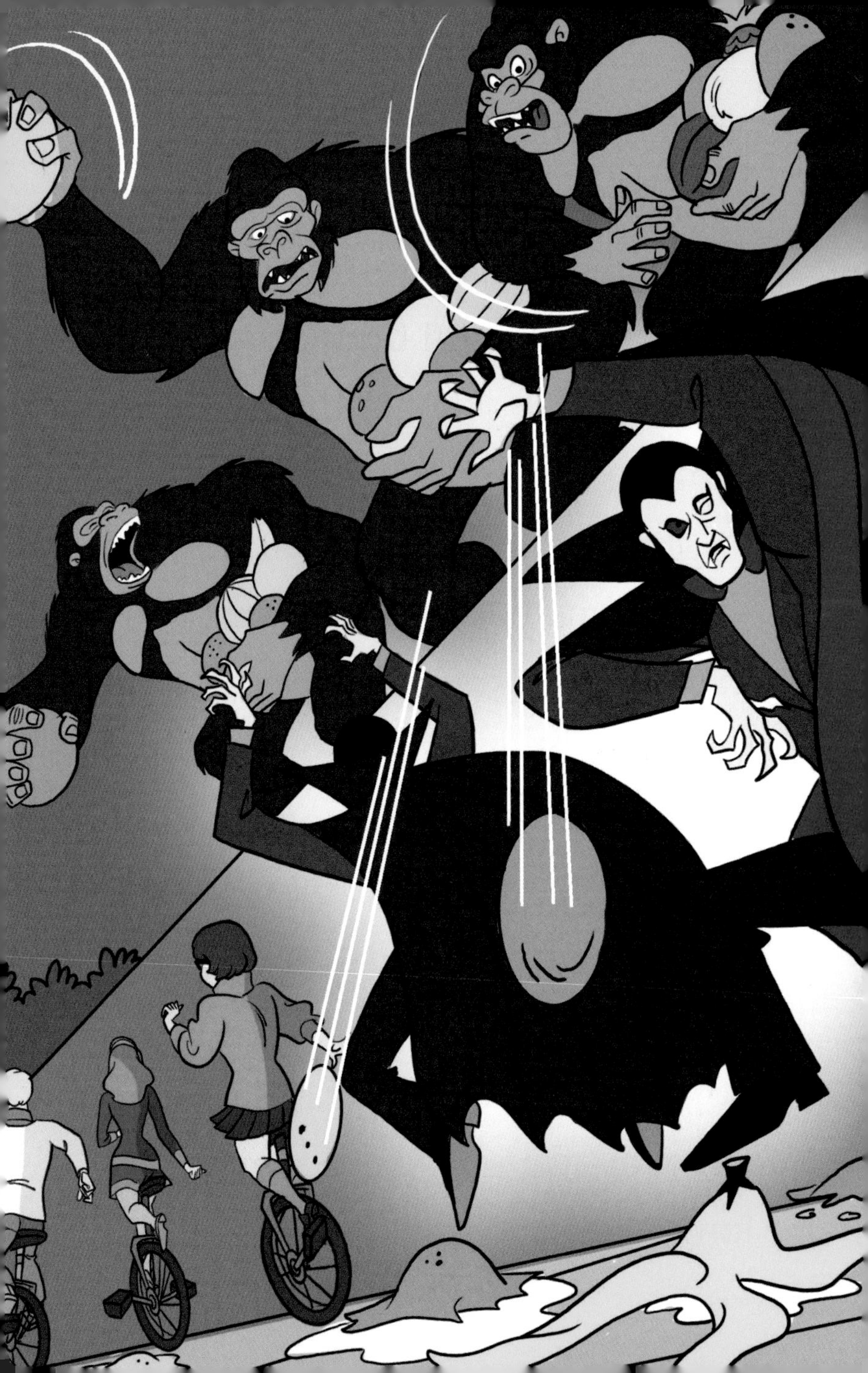

The gang pedaled fast along the main trail. Daphne swerved in on a unicycle and joined them. "All set on my end," she announced.

"Perfect," said Fred. "Let's finish this once and for all!"

Daphne led the way toward the zoo entrance. The vampires flew closer as everyone passed under a long row of trees.

Something moved in the branches above them.

Daphne looked up. "Your turn, Rocco!"

The trees above exploded with black spider monkeys. They swung down from the branches and landed on the vampires.

The monsters waved their arms, but the monkeys clung tight.

"Okay, gang," said Fred. "Clear out!"

The Mystery Inc. gang swerved out of the way. Up ahead, Scott slid a small ramp in front of one of the handrails. He ducked out of the way just as the monkey-covered vampires came close. The monsters hit the ramp and flew up and over into the pit.

"Great job, Rocco!" said Daphne. She gave the little monkey a high-five.

Scooby-Doo and the gang sprinted to the railing and peered over. Inside the pit, Bobo the bear was chasing the two vampires. The vampires floated in circles while Bobo pedaled his unicycle after them.

"Help!" shouted one of the vampires.

"Back, Bobo!" shouted the other. "Back!"

"Like, they don't sound like vampires to me," said Shaggy.

"Ruh-uh," agreed Scooby-Doo.

Just then, Bobo snagged one of the vampires' flowing robes.

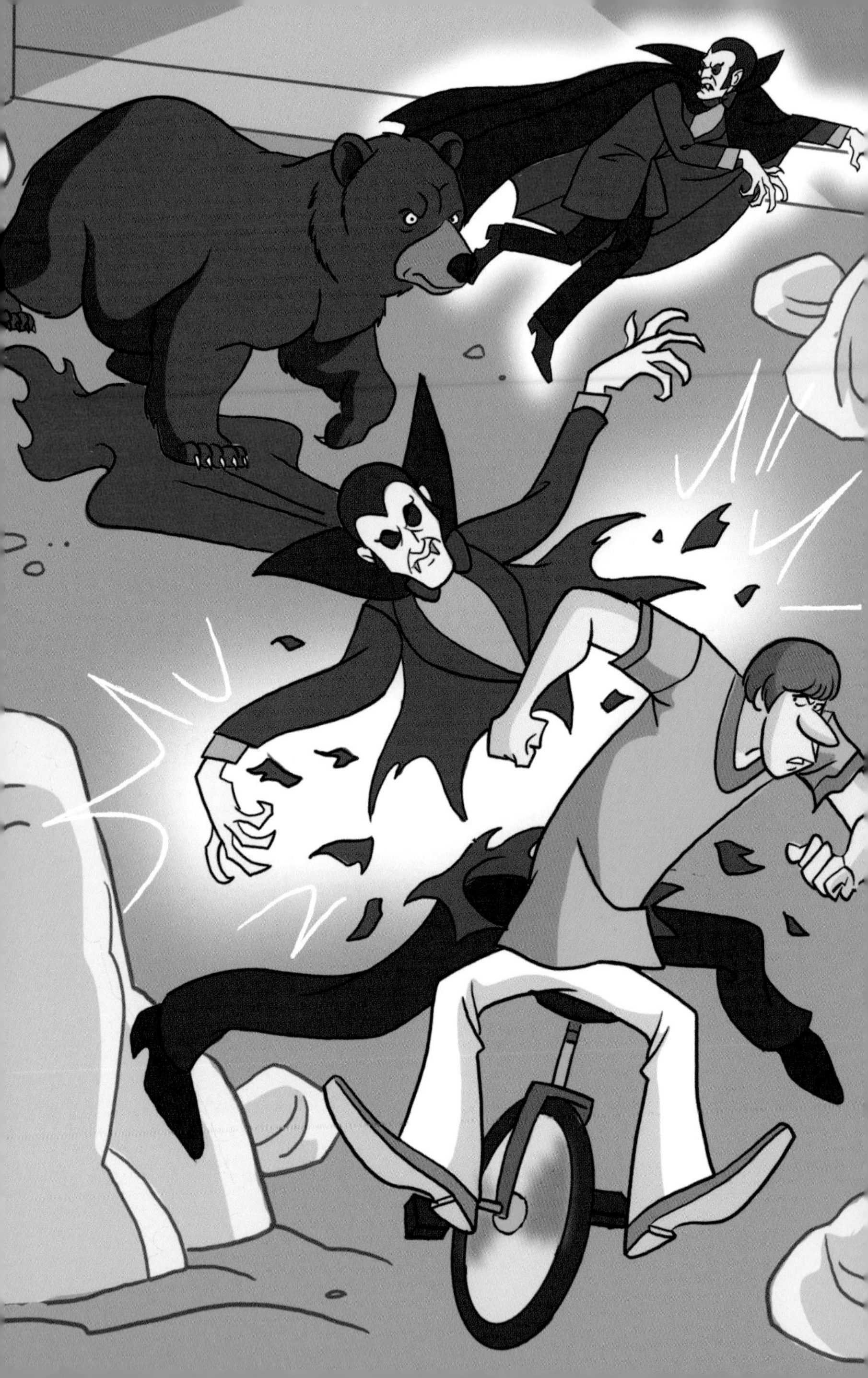

The robe ripped away showing a man riding a unicycle underneath.

"And these vampires can't really fly," said Daphne. "Their robes hid the unicycles they're riding."

"A-ha! That's where all the tire tracks came from," said Velma.

"Help!" shouted one of the vampires.

"We give up!" shouted the other. "We give up!"

Scott swung a rope ladder over the edge of the railing. The vampires ditched their unicycles and leaped for the ladder. They climbed out of the pit and collapsed on the ground.

"Tie them up, boys," said Daphne.

Rocco and a couple of other spider monkeys raced in. They wrapped long ropes around each vampire.

"Now, my favorite part," said Fred. "Unmasking the *villains*." He reached down and pulled the rubber vampire masks off each man.

"It's … " began Velma.

" … Barty and Billy Bohannon," finished Scott. "They owned the circus where I got many of my animals."

"You're the ones who mistreated all of those animals?" asked Daphne. "How awful."

"Mind your own business!" shouted Billy Bohannon. "We want our animals back!"

"And they stole the vampire bats so people would think two real vampires roamed the park," said Velma.

Fred held up the folded map. "They also marked the animals' locations on this zoo map."

"Well, you two will never harm another animal again. I'll make sure the police come and take you away," said Scott.

Barty frowned. "Ah … we would've gotten away with it too."

Barty nodded at one of the unicycles on the ground. "If it weren't for you pedaling, *meddling* kids."

Suddenly, a vampire poked its head out of a nearby bush.

"Zoinks!" Shaggy jumped into Velma's arms and whimpered. "Like, don't look now!" He pointed to the vampire face. "I think we missed a vampire!"

Scooby-Doo stepped out from the bush. He was wearing one of the rubber vampire masks. Scooby pulled it off and giggled. "Rooby-rooby-doo!"

THE END

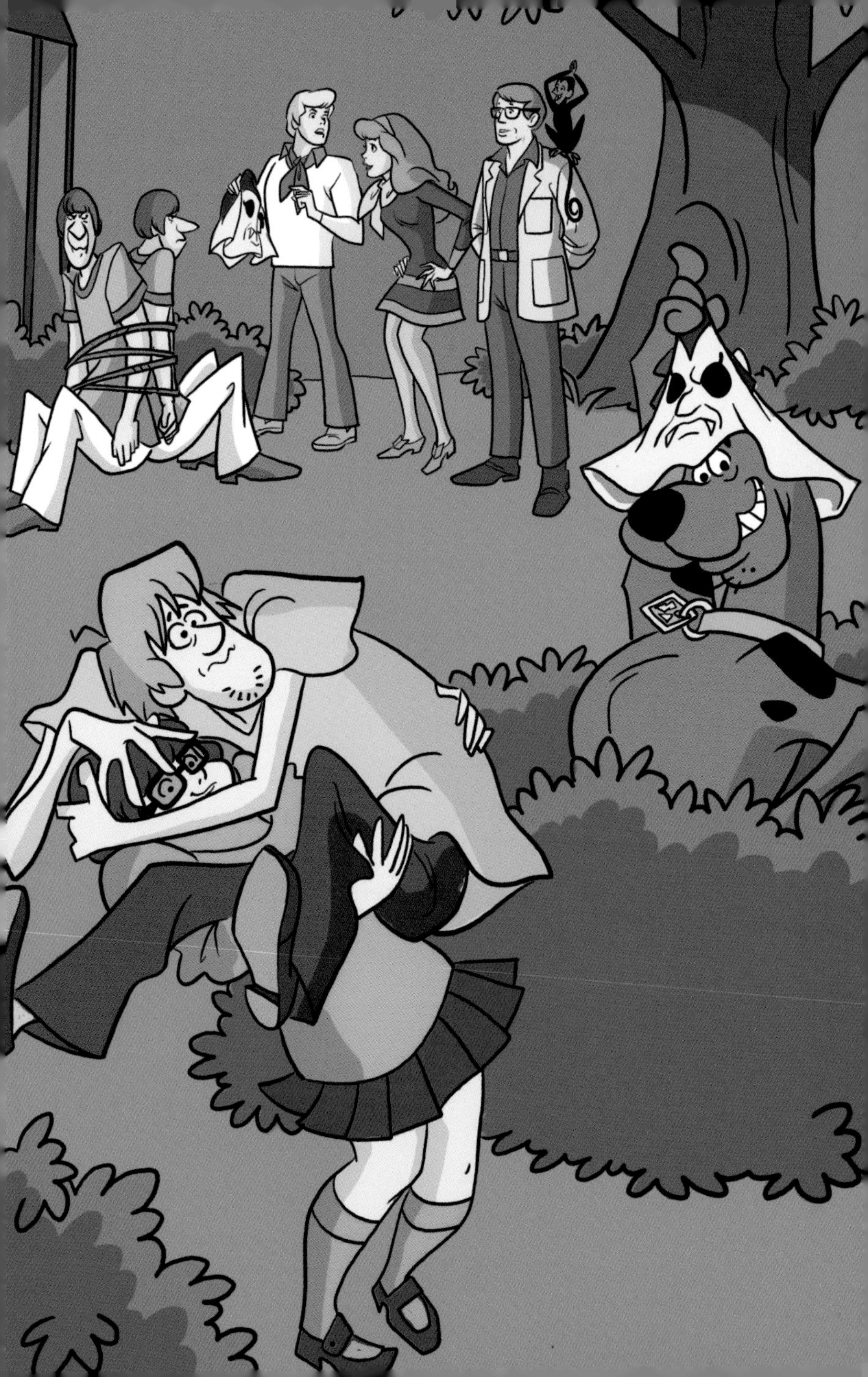

ABOUT THE AUTHOR

MICHAEL ANTHONY STEELE has been in the entertainment industry for more than 24 years writing for television, movies, and video games. He has authored more than one hundred books for exciting characters and brands, including Batman, Green Lantern, Shrek, LEGO City, Spider-Man, Tony Hawk, Word Girl, Garfield, Night at the Museum, and The Penguins of Madagascar. Mr. Steele lives on a ranch in Texas but he enjoys meeting his readers when he visits schools and libraries all over the country. He can be contacted through his website, MichaelAnthonySteele.com

ABOUT THE ILLUSTRATOR

SCOTT JERALDS has created many a smash hit, working in animation for companies including Marvel Studios, Hanna-Barbera Studios, M.G.M. Animation, Warner Bros., and Porchlight Entertainment. Scott has worked on TV series such as *The Flintstones, Yogi Bear, Scooby-Doo, The Jetsons, Krypto the Superdog, Tom and Jerry, The Pink Panther, Superman,* and *Secret Saturdays,* and he directed the cartoon series *Freakazoid,* for which he earned an Emmy Award. In addition, Scott has designed cartoon-related merchandise, licensing art, and artwork for several comic and children's book publications.

GLOSSARY

BAIT (BAYT)—food used as a trap for catching animals

BINOCULARS (buh-NAH-kyuh-luhrz)—a tool that makes faraway objects look closer

BOMBARD (bom-BAHRD)—to attack a person or place with heavy objects or gunfire

COSTUME (KOSS-toom)—clothes people wear to hide who they are

DESERTED (di-ZUHRT-uhd)—empty of people

DISTRACT (dis-TRAKT)—to draw attention away from something

EXHIBIT (ig-ZI-buht)—a display that shows something to the public

MISTREAT (miss-TREET)—to treat roughly, cruelly, or badly

RAMP (RAMP)—a slanted surface that joins two levels

STORAGE (STOR-ij)—a place where things are kept until they are needed

VILLAIN (VIL-uhn)—a wicked, evil, or bad person who is often a character in a story

DISCUSSION QUESTIONS

1. Do you like to go to the zoo? What do you like most about it? What is your favorite animal at the zoo?

2. The Mystery Inc. gang got help from different animals at the zoo. If you could be any kind of animal, what would you be? Why?

3. Vampires can be spooky make-believe monsters. Can you invent your own make-believe monster? Can you come up with a silly monster too?

WRITING PROMPTS

1. Write about the last time you visited the zoo. Describe the different animals you saw and what they were like.

2. Scooby-Doo and the gang got to ride fun unicycles. Write about a circus trick you would like to do.

3. Come up with your very own Scooby-Doo adventure! Write about the clues the Mystery Inc. gang would find and how they would solve the mystery.

LOOK FOR MORE

SCOOBY-DOO!

BEGINNER MYSTERIES